The House of Memory

DAVID CITINO

Ohio State University Press
Columbus

Library of Congress Cataloging-in-Publication Data

Citino, David, 1947–
The house of memory / David Citino.
p. cm.
ISBN 0-8142-0510-0 (alk. paper).
ISBN 0-8142-0513-5 (pbk : alk. paper).
I. Title.
PS3553.I86H6 1990 89-27188
811'.54—dc20 CIP

∞

The paper in this book meets the guidelines
for permanence and durability of the
Committee on Production Guidelines for Book
Longevity of the Council on Library Resources.

Printed in the U.S.A.

9 8 7 6 5 4 3 2 1

The House of Memory

FOR MARIA,

bella ragazza

CONTENTS

5. *The House of Memory*

ACKNOWLEDGMENTS

I wish to acknowledge, with thanks to their editors, the following magazines, in which these poems first appeared.

The Antioch Review: "The Fathers"

The Beloit Poetry Journal: "The Singer," "Rita Hayworth over Hiroshima"

The Centennial Review: "Watching Nightly News with the Sound Turned Down," "Staking the Garden"

The Chariton Review: "Meditation, during Another Hostage Crisis, on Randomness at the Subatomic Level"

Cincinnati Poetry Review: "M.S.," "Reviews," "Developers Announce Plans for Largest Shopping Mall in the Nation"

Cream City Review: "Ballad of the Northland Mall," "On His Daughter's Second Birthday," "The Father and the Son"

The Critic: "The Server," "The House of Memory," "A Religious History of Naples"

The Dalhousie Review: "St. Cassian of Imola, Writing Teacher and Martyr"

Gambit Magazine: "Fifty Years on the B&O, and Grandfather Gets a Watch"

Larry's Poetry Review: "Another Mexico"

Laurel Review: "The First Poem"

Light Year '86: "The Family in the Suburbs: A Situation Comedy"

The Literary Review: "Homage to Hildegarde of Bingen," "The Man with the Loud Mind," "Familiar as Home"

Menomonie Review: "Found Personals"

Mississippi Valley Review: "A Letter from Merton"

Modern Poetry Studies: "Arsenius, Who Had the Gift of Tears"

New Letters: "The Cremations"

The Journal: "Found Memo: Procedures Relating to the Death of a Student"

Poetry: "Charcoal Sketch of Aged Couple in Peasant Dress, Circa 1880," "In the Kitchen, He Recalls a Passage from Suetonius"

Poetry Northwest: "Basic Writing, Marion Correctional," "Starting the Garden, I Remember that the Citizens of Purgatory Knew Dante Was Alive because He Cast a Shadow"

Prairie Schooner: "The Man Who Couldn't Believe"

Salmagundi: "Poem to My Sons on the Feast of St. Simon of Crépy," "At the Hotel Giotto," "Journey to Calabria"

Seneca Review: "Going Downtown to Draw Up Our Will"

Shenandoah: "Thomas Edison Writes to Madame Elena Blavatsky, 1878"

South Dakota Review: "The Politics of Falling"

The Southern Review: "One Hundred Percent Chance of Snow, Accumulating Six to Eight Inches by Morning," "The News," "The Muscle of God," "Hiding the Skeleton"

Southern Humanities Review: "Opening Byron's Tomb, 1938"

St. Andrews Review: "The Statues"

Tar River Poetry: "In Drumcliff Churchyard," "Walking in the Piazza San Marco, I Remember Ascension of Our Lord Elementary, and Lester Shelton, Who Wore the Same Clothes Every Day"

The Yale Review: "Redwing"

I also wish to thank the National Endowment for the Arts for granting me a Creative Writing Fellowship in Poetry for 1986, and the Ohio Arts Council for an Individual Artist Major Fellowship for 1989–90.

1. *Rita Hayworth over Hiroshima*

THE SINGER

This is God's voice!
Mario Lanza on his deathbed,
grabbing at his throat

Those Italian boys, raised on the pitch
of her voice and a distant father's ravings
about his own goddess, the last great war,
memories real as dream, thick as Sunday sauce,
tart as vinegar, sweat between breasts
after sex—they do love their mothers.

Born Alfredo above father's produce store
the year Caruso died, he took her name,
Maria Lanza, first and maiden,
to get between her and the hairy ogre
who'd gotten to her first. *O sole mio.*

Sundays, all of South Philly turned out
to hear him make a spectacle of himself,
an art of praying. *Ave Maria, gratia plena.*

Booted out of school for sucker-punching
the Irish coach who'd called him *Wop,*
he'd fight any young hood he thought
was ogling her, still small and dark-eyed,
when the two of them went shopping,
holding hands and laughing like lovers.

She worked two jobs then, to help him
chase skirts and scores—though
he never had to chase them far,
to hear him tell it. He sent his wife
to the movies when Mamma came to call.
Be my love, for no one else
can end this yearning.

He'd stand like an oldtime fighter
when he sang, a Jersey shore bully boy,
chest outthrust, feet apart,
a perfect balance, in those early days,
between flesh and something like the soul.
Couldn't act a lick, but who
with an ear ever gave a damn?

He claimed that, one day in the studio
recording "Beloved," he came,
and there were times it seemed every note
was that spasm of pleasure that drives
a body out of itself: *When I'm singing*
it comes right out of my balls.

They fattened him to 240 for recording,
drove him back to 185 when it came time to film.
He couldn't see himself in any mirror.
MGM put him in a girdle toward the end.

In Italy, where it's theater to see
any grand past decay, and always
there's room for the one last tragedy,
it wasn't the custom to embalm.
For three days in the Roman villa
steamy as her kitchen, laid out
for the packed house of weepers
come to gasp and jeer at death's baby face,
mouth open as if for the highest C,
he rose like Mamma's Easter bread.

The undertaker had to crack
his shoulders and ankles, so small
was the coffin made by that one voice.

Still, though he's thin now
as a plastic disk, tinny in fake stereo,
I hear him call, a want beyond
the time and blare of day,
beauty we're made to carry inside
splashing like Chianti
in a flash of brilliance,
the aging bone when it's touched
whining like fine crystal,
and I think how good it can be,
this need to sing to those we love.

RITA HAYWORTH OVER HIROSHIMA

How quickly history becomes our footage,
newsreel loop screened over and over.
We mean to speak, and William the Conqueror
crosses the Channel with a boatload
of our own words, aching for a fight.
Take *plague,* for example, the one
the *Little Boy* dropped on Hiroshima,
which still falls from the *Enola Gay,*
Rita Hayworth's photograph taped
to its pitiless girth,
the captive Rita whistling down, down, forever
pouty, supple, and uncorrupted.
At the same moment *Voyager One* moves out
from the solar system toward the end
of everything, bearing figures
of naked Eve and Adam,
and the voice
of U.N. Secretary General Kurt Waldheim
caught on a gold record, repeating
again and again in thick English
I send greetings on behalf
of the people of our planet.
Below, our parents are still bound
to their bed, performing a dance
without end, our lives
their twitching urgency,
one sperm carrying 23 chromosomes
slapping and struggling like a salmon

toward one egg with its own 23,
merely to become us,
their breathlessness our inspiration,
panting gasps our song,
their rising and falling on the mattress
even this moment creaking out our time.
I have proof here in my hand,
a photograph taken before I was.
It's 44 years later and she's still radiant
in Father's pinup nailed to palm trunk
at jungle's edge near Henderson Field
on bloody Guadalcanal, lithely long-limbed,
coy smile shimmering like the morning star:
the incomparable Rita Hayworth.

IN DRUMCLIFF CHURCHYARD

Cast a cold eye
on life, on death.
Horseman, pass by.

At the grave of Yeats
irreverent, raucous rooks
lumber from oak-tops to the tip
of Drumcliff church and back again
in a straight line. No widening gyres,
they're too heavily of this world,
wings flapping like backyard laundry.
I've come from Lissadell House,
where for 50 pence the niece
of the Countess flopped before me
in soiled tennis shoes
and told well-rehearsed tales
of a poet plagued night after night
by ghosts who couldn't understand
his later verse. Now this tomb
under Ben Bulben, worn-out myth
on the horizon, going nowhere forever.
Nailed to the tree nearby, the sign,
    Feel like a sandwich?
    Visit the Yeats Tavern.
I know how I'm supposed to feel,
and fight the panic climbing
down into my lungs, noose
about the throat, the singer's mouth

stuffed with Irish earth that I put
to my lips and taste Ohio.
There are words here
I know better than my own,
fumble in a greasy till,
bee-loud glade,
a tattered coat upon a stick,
a terrible beauty.
Say what you will
about the hoary politics and ghouls.
Beneath the chuckling birds
there's stillness rooted in rock and peat,
a beauty sweet and bitter
as blood on the tongue,
chilly art of the eternal.
Turning back to this world, this day,
I know I'm leaving something
more precious than my life.

THOMAS EDISON WRITES TO MADAME ELENA BLAVATSKY, 1878

Knowing? It's history,
My Dear Teacher, coming
from worlds rarer than ours,
ideas like light streaming
into stained windows
of the cathedral of skull.

One lifetime? The dropcloth
of memory, My Wisdom;
age a blow to the head,
the great amnesia machine,
memory leaking out to seek new hosts,
flammable as oil.

All last night, Love,
I sat in the lab, copper coil wound
like bandages around my head, trying
to invent what others feel,
telepathy of genius. Nothing
came of it, but I know

we're electric, My Creativity,
every thought a fire
real as disembodied voices
spinning from every silence,
figures twining on the wall,
light at once where darkness ruled.

OPENING BYRON'S TOMB, 1938

His sexual organ shewed quite abnormal development.
A. E. Houldsworth, People's Warden
of St. Hucknall Parish Church

The unlettered village men, smoking
and joking anxiously, slowly lower
by rope a miner's lamp to try
history's caustic atmosphere,
giving chaos a redeemed sense of place.
Feet and legs, torso and head,
each drops into this dusty, musty hell.
The desecration, performed to thrill
a literary vicar, unearths other crime:
name plate, velvet coverlet, brass cherubs,
urns that bore liver and heart
all missing, evidence that nothing
in life leaves a body more vulnerable
than taking leave. Death itself
isn't always the worst of crimes.
The warden lists what's been stolen,
knowing he'll never get it said.
And then they lift coffin lids
of iron, brass and finished wood
and shine their lights on a lover
blooming where all ultimately are planted.
He's not himself—quite right—
but he's no one else, the poet laboring
at the last lyric masterpiece,
timeless lines of the purest truth and lie.

POEM TO MY SONS ON THE FEAST OF ST. SIMON OF CRÉPY

He desired to be a monk, moved thereto . . . by
the sight of the decomposing body
of his father which he was taking to be buried.

Taps, fountainheads, drip and drop, sons.
Life leaks out. Moments seep and ooze.
Anything put up? Made to plummet: leaf and stalk,
tegument and limb, bone after bone.
We can't all deny ourselves behind trees
like Merton in his cultivated Kentucky.

Our days fill us up to overflowing. Osmosis.
Evaporation. Agues and agues of entropy.
Take heart, my children. This father,
the one who tried to teach you how
to stand in woods like a man to return
to earth what water you took, to feel

pride in the great arc of shining youth;
to reverence life so much you'd strive
to rid the room of flies by trusting
the eye, snatching them from air
to be released beyond the door uncrushed;
who meant to show that holiness means

knowing what to do with your hands
through every moment of labor and play:
he isn't, you see, what he was. Remember?
This proves that neither will you be.
Permit him to teach by example how to fail,
hating all the while this decomposition.

It's devotion, I'm saying, your memories must be.

ARSENIUS, WHO HAD THE GIFT OF TEARS

. . . the tears which he had shed continually
had worn away his eye-lashes.

Tears retouch the portrait of a life.
What's sordid grows less so, the lovely
more, softened by sorrow's rain.
Did you mourn for the immortal mosaics
of the Palace, the gold you earned
tutoring the Emperor's sons out of
the happiness of their unlearning?
Or was it the stinking monks you joined
after God shouted you out of the world
of the rich? What were you trying,
to cry away the finely lying past,
each night's blindness? You lifted
your arms from sunfall to rising
in a cross of bony flesh, your offering
of forty years of bad bread
on a chiaroscuro desert, and insults
from the boorish brothers who hooted
at the dainty manners you'd learned
seated at the right hand of popes.
Why so many tears, Brother?

I'm learning the language of saints,
each letter an ache caught deep
in the throat, life a sentence
unpronounceable except by weeping,
this weather of the heart,
roar and suck of the parent wind and sea,
bellow of the wounded beast of us,
our most human song.

ST. CASSIAN OF IMOLA, WRITING TEACHER AND MARTYR

Professor, even at the end,
carried away by your own passion
for perfection, you would be heard,
droning on in the steamy courtroom
while distant dogs and vendors
tolled the day away. The judge,
ex-army political appointment
who'd seen, through too many campaigns,
the mortal danger of rhetoric, a man
with no love for those whose hearts
hemorrhage at the mystery
and preach the potential divinity
of every rank and file, was bored
as could be, having heard hundreds
before you dying to profess
the unity of creation, weeping
that all must agree.
He'd somewhere else to be hours ago,
and still you ranted on
about inspiration, conception, the Word.
He sentenced you to die, but not
in any of the trite ways—
no barbs from illiterate gladiators
or lion fangs honed keen
on human gristle and bone.
He ordered your students
to stab you with their styluses.

A bad class after all,
they were too happy to oblige,
hating you for your stinging insistence
on the spirit and law of letters.
Even as you fell finally silent,
you made them, in bold strokes
still red, tell something
of that pure embellishment
of mind and heart we call the truth.

A LETTER FROM MERTON

The way from Eden to my Gethsemane
leads through Kentucky.
I've named each tree and weed,
living like Simon of Kent
whose hermitage for twenty years
was a hollow oak, or the desert fathers
who rode palm trees from star to star.
This deep in thought even awful Mars
hangs like a little red fruit
from the topmost branch of silver maple.
I'm so far gone it took Hiroshima
twelve months to find me.
It was here, alone, I learned
to grow, planting my sins
in a Zen garden. Speaking in signs,
I learned to sing, the notes
rising light as finches to settle
in rows of justified type,
inspired fields. Monks
aren't born; they're made
by severe mothers, expiring fathers.
Is there one word that can make
a woman or man a saint? *No.*
Here there are no businessmen,
though in August the flies
I've sworn never to harm hurt
nearly as bad. Solitude, I've found,
never comes tomorrow, or in some

other place. It's the deepening
of the river of here and now,
each instant rushing like spring currents
to carry the rooted one away.
Eternity happens this moment.
In hollows of the soul, nothing's louder
than the will. All life means
learning to be still. I've learned
there's no seeing but what
can be imagined in the deepest night,
no hearing but cries of sex
from every flower.

HOMAGE TO HILDEGARDE OF BINGEN

And I saw a great swamp, over which hung a black cloud
of smoke. . . . And in the swamp there swarmed a mass
of little worms. Here were the souls of those who in
the world had delighted in foolish merriment.

I grew up before the abolition of hell,
Hildegarde. Your sentences hurt infinitely more
than writing a thousand times *I must*
not talk or the name my parents made
in their furtive thrashings through dark
or paddlings from Jesuits. You promised smoke
fouler than Cleveland winds blowing
through open windows of St. Ignatius
from the Cuyahoga valley, stench worse
than the West Side slaughterhouse
that left me breathless August nights,
the river red as something out of Bosch,
burning bright as U.S. Steel's forge.
The worst horror, the Sisters of Mercy
tried to convince us, would be
never seeing the face of God.
The fire would crackle for all time
yet never consume the flesh,
I learned on the first night of retreat.
If my own mother made it into heaven
she'd be too happy staring at God
to mourn for me writhing below.
Not even the wasteland outside

the fallout shelter downtown—where
we'd get by on surplus crackers and hardtack
until the red cloud drifted away—
would be as bad. Ashen as charcoal
in the spent censer after Benediction,
the senior boys lined up for Confession
before Mass on Monday mornings
after a weekend of drive-ins
and slow, slow dancing with girls
from Magnificat, and left the box
breathing deeply again, perfect angels
until the next open-mouthed kiss.
Nightmare was the body too heavy
to ascend to the realm of angels,
so swollen with love it could burst,
family stories of evil uncles who went down,
bellies fat with tumors big as eggplants.
There were nights I'd lay me down
convinced that before dawn
I'd break into flame to burn bright
as a Christmas tree. Fear
was the cold lover moving above me
night after night. Even now,
years from shadows cast
by High Mass candles, I feel
the flickering chill just behind
even the smallest happiness, though
I'm old enough to fear no hell
but what this adult world's become.

2. *The Politics of Falling*

THE POLITICS OF FALLING

1.

Just then, I felt it, the heart
squeezed briefly, a small pain
where I once placed the soul.
Somewhere near there's been a falling,
like the Wild-Irish-Rose-soaked derelict
stumbling in a blizzard
into the 4 A.M. drift past which
children will walk to and from school
that day and all winter long
until spring melts the snow
and thaws his fingers which will call out
to them. Looking in his still-clear eye
they'll scream, and running home
in their first terror, fall and fall again.

2.

So many days, so many years
of this life consumed. Where
are the breaths I took unheeding,
blessings taken for granted,
this heart through it all
booming loud as an Ohio woodlot
teeming with deer hunters
the first week in December,
stags and pregnant does falling into snow,
wounds in their flanks
red as the fake carnations
sold by Disabled American Veterans
on Memorial Day?

3.

The doors of the poor, paint
festering, thresholds splintered,
wood warped and worn from the unwashed hands
of hard, hard years, tenement walls
of the Third World falling
from earthquake and despair
to make room for contemporary cathedrals,
breathtaking skyline art,
glass and shining spires of foreign banks.

4.

The city oppresses like war
some days, comes close
to stopping the heart.
On the tongue and breasts
of a woman who's come breathless
from a distant side of town
through wet streets thick
with the blue and acrid pall of commerce
to remove her blouse
and fall with me
to the floor cold
as the shut-down forge of U.S Steel:
the taste of Diesel fumes.

5.

I make a fist. Inside
there's the darkness
that lives inside my mother's breast,
arteries slowly closing
around my father's heart,
soul of this dying Rustbelt city,
the space just six feet deep
and the size of my body
which, once I fall,
never again will see the light.

WATCHING NIGHTLY NEWS
WITH THE SOUND TURNED DOWN

This one's just tweedy and gray enough
to be trustworthy, cardigan
under the conservative jacket to show
he's got the common touch, and cares
whether or not I have a nice day.
He must be a star, his face takes up
so much screen. I see the line
around the neck where makeup ends.
At times the concerned visage
and choreographed lips are replaced
by other scenes. A jet in flames
plummets like Icarus into a silent sea.
Sad-eyed men, shoulders sagging
from some terrible weight,
gather menacingly in broad daylight,
hands gesturing fast as sparrows.
Factories lie empty; meeting halls are full.
Women in shapeless black raise arms to me
as if in prayer. One lifts what seems
at first a bundle of sticks, charred dark
as stormcloud, but as the camera moves in
I see the tiny limbs and face.
Old men wearing great suits
sit around polished tables cluttered
with papers. All seem to be
talking at once, even as they pose
for the cameras. Nodding wisely,

lab-coated doctors and scientists
hold up aerosol cans and bottles of pills.
Families come together
around enormous cereal boxes
before dissolving into darkness.
Automobiles are driven breathlessly
around the Rockies by lovely women
who slowly lick their lips and shift
their long legs. Charts, graphs,
minus and plus, lines rising slowly
or plunging in red to the very bottom.
At last there are no more flags,
bloated bellies, fists, fists, fists.
The man stops opening and closing
his mouth. He smiles. His eyes
are deep blue. *I understand how*
you must feel, he seems to say.
His teeth gleam the whitest white.
News of an average day, but
I must never forget the thousand words
each nightly picture's worth.
It's this silence, after all, that kills.

DEVELOPERS ANNOUNCE PLANS FOR LARGEST SHOPPING MALL IN THE NATION

The things of light we've eclipsed
with this careening velocity, bloodiest mass,

mind of the spider dew-jeweled at dawn
across our noisy, blundering way,

blessings we're given, soft milkweed seed,
while we plod along loud as firecrackers

flung into empty dumpsters. Too busy
to perceive, much less give thanks for,

we've become the heavy in each day's plot,
thunderers blasting pine twig, gnat and ant,

spores borne on Ohio woodlot winds, pheromones
seeping out to whisper *Love, O love*. We breathe

near spring-cold streams and furrowed fields
and suddenly thousands of perfect creatures—

heirs to all of time—give up the ghost.
How many more before we expire, too gross even

for earth? What weight, these wants we lie and say
are needs, every damn minute another bright idea.

BASIC WRITING,
MARION CORRECTIONAL

I come each day through fields
furrowed with corn, bean and barbed wire
overseen by moonlighting farmers
perched in watchtowers, cheeks pink,
shotguns cocked to cultivate their order.
In the Visitors' Lounge the women
wait, weary from the bus ride
from Cleveland or Toledo, skirts slit
over best hose over legs new-shaven,
lips forcing smiles cold
as institutional porcelain.
In the corner a couple entwines,
his leg between hers, his hands
working beneath her blouse,
their children trying not to see.
The guard who frisks me jokes the same
each day: *You got anything in there*
but poems, Doc? I walk past The Hole
and see men come out, eyes wild
with crazy static. In the Job Readiness Room
they're all in jeans and work shirts
like my English-major classmates
at Ohio U in 1969. All chain smoke
but the Muslims. They want to know
about my wife. *What color hair?*
She make you happy? You got a picture?
I tell them about comma faults.

Delivery-van doors slam gunshot-loud outside,
jerk them from their seats.
The loudspeaker thunders above my words:
C Block, Chow. Work Call: Yard Gang,
Shop Gang, Laundry Gang, Sanitation Gang.
It was coke, speed, horse
that put us here, they write, bad crowds
we ran with, bad men that hustled
our mothers, The Man who jerked us around.
I help them with their letters.
O my precious lady I ache
for the righteous mysteries of your thighs.
Dear Honey I got something I been saving up
for you. Dear Most Gracious Ladies and Gentlemen
of the Parole Board: I've changed my life.
With their pencils they want to shake
the Governor. I'm magic as a preacher,
they believe, because of words,
because each night I sleep beside a woman
and each day I've leave to touch
a son's cheeks soft as petals
of a courtyard rose rising beyond
shadows of all four walls.
They yearn to soar above cinder blocks
of each lethal year, hearts constricting
in barred cells of the breast,
hands into fists. This makes nothing
better, all admit. We're waiting
for the bell, summons from a purer world.
Time's the law, the hell men do.

ANOTHER MEXICO

The world's population climbed to 4.9 billion in 1985, adding 85 million—the equivalent of another Mexico.
Associated Press

It's an endless, halting parade.
He rides the armored Popemobile
through tortuous Third World streets
rife with need, birdlike cries
of wanters, wishers—believers all.

The suspension of procreation,
he tells them, *must never*
be brought about by artificial,
and therefore immoral, means.
Control yourselves, my little ones.

Heaven's coming for those
who know discipline and abnegation.
After he passes, the children
lie down in fetid urban mud,
flies whispering about their eyes.

The Catholic side of Cleveland, even,
after the war. I recall that for all
our Western waste and wealth,
alleys, avenues and church pews
grew thick with children,

mothers going devoutly crazy
under the great weight of husbands,
rhythms of beautiful bawling babies
month upon aching month. Burdens
of joy, Cleveland after Cleveland,

Delhi, Rio, the whole world slowing
with the weight, tenements and shacks
of sex, only so much love to go around.
Now, this miraculous catastrophe
in a single year: another Mexico.

MEDITATION, DURING ANOTHER HOSTAGE CRISIS, ON RANDOMNESS AT THE SUBATOMIC LEVEL

Dream as we might
that there's an azure round
for every taloned raptor's arc,
and each moon's beauty
troubles precisely these mortal seas,
today we must take on faith
a random universe,
fields of cause without effect,
theories of chaos.
One impossible electron,
particle and wave,
spins both here and there.
Neither time nor space can mean.
One hundred million neutrinos
pass through my hand
even now as it makes
its uncertain way across
this page. The strong force
and the weak keep us together
even as we're torn apart by science.
What brought our distant kinfolk,
horny for martyrdom, weeping
to their bloody knees
at the mouth of the cave

moves me now as I consider
the gun thrust against
one guiltless skull,
a body dumped on the tarmac.
If God's been blown to bits
in the Big Bang, who
rains on us? Our laws
etched in stone decree
a pure uncertainty.
The one truth as we breathe
our brief eternities?
That we must sometimes burn
for parents' sins. The one fear?
That we may wake tomorrow
to find only what we are,
and in all the natural universe
no reason at all.

THE CREMATIONS

Land for the Living,
the bumper sticker proclaims,
one slogan it's hard to argue with.
We're running out of earth,
mound on mound and slab by slab.
After all, the winds
were made to prevail.
To rise, we learn, can be holy,
to lift like purple finches into song.
It's mortal sin to sink
to piles of compost smoldering
long after our time,
buried life after life.
We can be so swiftly elemental,
light as the song that bursts
from the milkweed pod.
Walk outside. Look up.
It's Mother. Father.
They float like archangels
high above the Tetons,
Sangre de Cristos and Alleghenies,
spin like twisters up and down
the prairie borne on wings
of housefly, gnat, and Monarch,
circle Midway and O'Hare,
settle gently to consecrate fields
of flowering bean and tasseled corn,
lovers moving together along the beach.

Our children are stained
with their scents.
Their voices hiss and roar
from any flame.
They pass through our very souls,
damn and praise us
from petal, blade and leaf,
our inspiration.

M.S.

There's nothing you won't stand for?
Nerves sputter, flickering out
like a bad string of Christmas lights
all up and down your girth.
Slick fingers pinch flames
back to their wicks. *Hiss.*
Wife and mother cry out, hands
clutching mouths, children avoiding

your eyes. Some collision grating
loud as concrete on chrome
might be more to your liking?
A mortal stroke? Anything but
this comedy, the stumbling body,
your royal numbness, dazzling virtuoso
gone all thumbs, fish-limp,
clumsy as a clownish oldster

hot for somebody young as May,
both of them breathless—
but he for all the wrong reasons—
balance now his only passion.
Flesh gone slumbering. Limbs twitch,
needles and pins, bloodless prick
on thickest skin. So, so tired.
It hits you just like this,

the resonant world gone to static.
The final uprightness of your days
abruptly leaning, coal tipple
precarious on Appalachian cliff.
Dizzy, dizzy. Two left feet
on buffed-wax dance floor.
Mail unopened. Not taking calls.
A body learning its own uselessness.

THE STATUES

A dream of walking statues.
I see the loveliest citizens of Delphi,
five hundred priceless bronzes,
moving toward crazy Rome and Nero,
gods, satyrs, heroes, nymphs
trundled on the conquerors' carts,

silent tribe with arms upraised
as if they stood as witnesses
to the fading eternity of the body.
They're driven toward the setting sun,
heads bobbing behind shanks
of the empire's relentless oxen.

When Constantinople topples Rome
the statues are marched back
through Greece to the East, some
to be lost forever, others to take
to the road again, to be wheeled
by caretakers into a thousand museums.

Or San Nicola, stolen from Asia Minor
by Bari fishermen a thousand years ago,
once nimble as any child, now old enough
to need to be carried to water's edge
from his cathedral to bless the fleet,
streets careening with devout shouts.

Back in Cleveland's Little Italy,
The Virgin moves down Murray Hill
above a crowd of dark-eyed *paesans,*
one thousand crisp bills pinned
to her cape to astound the crowd.
Myself, it all comes back to, at ten,

gold-embroidered cope over my shoulders
as I carry the heavy Byzantine icon,
Our Lady of Perpetual Help, down
the center aisle of Ascension of Our Lord.
How I feared a misstep, recalling
Uzzah, hapless teamster walking in awe

beside the Ark of the Covenant,
crushed suddenly by the shifting cargo
of a terrible God. Myself turning
cold as moss-dark, rain-swept stone
as the neurologist interprets for me
this art, blownup photo of my brain

in shades and hues that shimmer
soft as Impressionist fields and ponds
under institutional light, lesions
grave-dark riddling the light,
patches of eroded myelin, dead nerve,
the neurologist speaking of wheelchairs.

3. *The Man with the Loud Mind*

THE MAN WITH THE LOUD MIND

Most of the time there were voices
from both sides of the brain, thoughts
like static, or the tone-arm dragged
scraping across amplified vinyl,
or cherry bombs detonated inside dumpsters,
but every so often his head would fill
with the voice of God
scored for concert orchestra and conducted
by George Szell. When he remembered
an old rhythm or riff, Little Richard
or Elvis or James Brown as he stood
on the platform waiting for a train,
hundreds near him began to dance
like Philly kids on Bandstand,
while his Cole Porter stuff set them
to hoofing it around him
like platinum chorines and stage-door Johnnys.
When words of love came back to him
the crowds hustling to work downtown
paired off and moved together
for all they were worth, down and dirty
in the street, on diner stool
and cathedral pew, back seats of taxis,
limos and pimp-mobiles, citizens
of the city of love moving to his wishes.
When he switched the channel
to some hoary country hymn he brought

the world to its knees, nations
of rugged crosses, speakers
in tongues, tear-jerkers wailing
like Hank or Merle of dead mommas
waiting up late for wayward sons
while reading from Good Books,
every chamber of every heart a chapel,
until like night coming down
hard as dirt dropped twelve feet
from the scoop of a growling backhoe
in a cemetery, his mind went blank,
and nothing, no one stirred,
and there were no more melodies,
not one blessed word.

THE MAN WHO COULDN'T BELIEVE

He was the sort who *entertained*
doubts. Even in early childhood
when his mother would call out
"Your daddy's home," he'd look up

from toys that were nothing more
than toys and, with a smile
both knowing and superior,
shake his head from side to side.

When Sister Mary Appassionata asked
"Why did God make you?"
he looked her straight in the eye.
"Damned if I know," he answered.

Even love was out of the question,
a series of motions out and in,
crescendo, diminuendo. "You're no worse
than the last one, and I need it,"

he'd calmly plead. "I do. I do."
It rained or shined on his parades
for meteorological reasons only.
Stars were there because they were.

Forget charmed quarks and neutrinos,
though he admitted that molecules
might exist. He could perceive
Brownian motion in the shudder

of maple leaf upon the river,
even though he suspected wind
as the rational explanation.
He found himself on earth

to consume and be consumed in turn,
to grow old and fill a hole
in some city cemetery. Afraid
of the unknown, the dark? No way.

He was all *I.* Heaven and hell
were this moment, this one, this.
He died as he lived, fearless
and alone. He didn't have a prayer.

FOUND PERSONALS

[With each tick and seep of blood and glands
we pray, in rows of justified type neat
as theater seats, that someone
with the ways and means to make us happy
listens, reads us diligently, takes us to heart.]

Desperately Need $500. Will Pay Back $1000 In 2 Weeks.

Dial-A-Miracle

Professional Massage. Sauna.
Body Shampoo. Open 7 Days A Week 24 Hours.
Women and Men. Licensed. Reputable.
(Adult Conversation. All Oriental Staff.)

Asleep Or Awake Pregnancy Termination. Early Test 24
Days From Last Period. Reduced Rates For ADC. Accent
On Caring. Confidential. Visa, Master, Or Discover Card.

Handsome Safe Adult Will Drive You
Or Your Car Anywhere You Wish.
References.

Free Heat Machine. Did Your Gas Bill Shock You?
This Amazing Unit Slips Into Your Fireplace And Heats
Your Home
Absolutely Free. Hurry. Only A Few Left.

Good News For Jews!!! (Recorded Message)

Fast Cash. Any Sum. Integrity Since 1976.

Where Are You? Beautiful Red-haired Girl Seated In Section 4 Row 42 Seat 48 At 7 P.M. Madonna Concert February 11. Call Me. I'm David. Remember?

Cure For Herpes And AIDS
Found In Old Testament.
Call Collect.

Lost License? Hit-Skip? DWI? Points?
We Insure Absolutely Anyone.

Adult Movie Motel. Clean Rooms. Privacy. No Questions Asked. Water Beds. Special Short Term Rates. Different Movies Hourly.

O Most Precious Sacred Heart of Jesus!
O Mary Terrible As An Army Dressed in Battle
Array! O Legba, Voodoo Jesus!

MWM With Poet's Soul 50 Yrs Old 5 Ft 6, 300 Lbs Seeks Hotblooded Willowy Educated Cultured WF 21–25. You Will Take The Place Of Mother And Virgin Goddess. I Will Be Your Love Slave During Lunch Hour Sessions Of Egalitarian Sharing And Sheer Abasement. You Are As Uncontrollably Passionate As You Are Discreet. I Will Do Anything You Demand No Matter How Distasteful. (Roman Catholic Democrat Non-Smokers Only Please.)

Ladies Invite Us To Your Next Home Party. A Presentation Of Sheer And Alluring Lingerie. Playthings For Grownups. Oils, Creams And Edible Underwear In Most Popular Flavors (Including New Pistachio and Pesto-Lite). Detailed Treasure Map To The G-Spot. Whips, Nipple Clips And Restraints For Fun And Recreation. Safe Battery Powered Aids That Don't Quit Until You Do. Exclusive Distributor Of Exer-Sexer Seat Of Love.

St. Jude of the Hopeless. St. Teresa.
St. Anthony. Colonel North.
St. Christopher. Dear Elvis.
Ora Pro Nobis.

I Love You Now And Forever. Please Reconsider. On And After This Date. Anyone Witnessing Accident. I've Been A Damn Fool. Call If You Still Care. You're Our Baby Girl. Our Only Son. I'm Sincere This Time. What's He Got I Don't? *Full Collection Nazi S.S. Regalia For Sale. Moving. Must Sell. Make Offer.* We Love You. Love You. Honest We Do. Please Come Home. Please Come Home. Please.

FOUND MEMO: PROCEDURES RELATING TO THE DEATH OF A STUDENT

The death of a student
is a serious and sad loss
to the University.

This loss is particularly keen
among family and friends
and a compassionate and timely response
is incumbent upon us.

In order to do this effectively
we must follow
a consistent and centralized set
of procedures and policies.

Essentially we ask that if
you become aware of the death
of a University student
you notify the Office of Student Services
(422-9334)

of as many details of the death
as you know.
This office will serve
as the central point of contact
for such reports

and will notify other University offices
as appropriate.

Although I sincerely hope
you will not have to invoke
these Procedures
I trust you will retain this memorandum
as a reminder
of them.

Should you wish to review them,
copies are filed in the offices
of the Vice Presidents, Deans,
and College Secretaries.

Thank you for your attention
and understanding.

THE FAMILY IN THE SUBURBS: A SITUATION COMEDY

I.

She bursts in on him
in the frigid garage, tools
hanging straight as a plumbline
from the pegboard, screwdrivers,
drill bits and wrenches
of every size, Toro mower
and snow blower side by side
behind the nine-passenger wagon.
Clad only in loincloth
and L. L. Bean hunting jacket
he's sitting on his haunches eating
a squirrel, blood-drops
red as cherries steaming in his beard,
bits of entrails, gristle and fur
stuck between teeth. Women
from some other side of town
dance around him in the latest
from Frederick's of Hollywood,
leather teddies and peek-a-boo bras,
spiked heels, garter belts and fishnet hose,
hair wild as untrimmed rosebushes
and matted with sweat,
eyes smoldering like cigarette-tips
in a honky-tonk just before closing.
"I can explain everything," he says.

2.

Lately he's spent all his time
in the garage, hammering, sawing,
screwing things. She takes baths.
One day her groans call him
into the house. He smashes
into the bathroom with the ball-peen hammer
he bought at Sears that very morning,
splintering the door just as the doll
squeezes from between her thighs
and floats on its back in the steamy water.
"Mama, Dada," it coos, each syllable
a bubble round as this earth
bearing heavenward their image together
and flames of the three scented K-Mart candles
blazing in tiny cups on the back
of the commode. "You're probably
the father," she tells him,
"I swear it on my mother's grave."
"It has my eyes!" he cries.

BALLAD OF THE NORTHLAND MALL

Wandering too far from lawns of home
she met a man browsing in Waldenbooks,
the section labeled *Mysterious and Occult.*

The wind seemed to rise all around him,
as if he stood darkly on a stormy moor.
His hair made her think of the birch trees

set in tubs at the center of the mall
beside the brimming fountain brilliant
with hues of red and white and blue

where ten thousand weekend shoppers
had wished their shiny dimes away.
Was it a telescoped umbrella he tapped

against his thigh, or some swelling shadow?
All that day they walked hand in hand
from Foxy Ladies of the 80's Boutique

to the Gourmet Cookie Shoppe, wound
a samba around the gartered mannequins
in Victoria's Secret as she blushed

like a Norman Rockwell bride, strolled
from Penney's to the other end
of everything—in this case, Sears.

Back in the bookstore he showed her
his favorite pages of *The Joy of Sex*
and a score of novels written by Anon.,

and within twelve nights each had fondled
the other's aroused dreams before
all screens of the Super Cinema Six.

He took her to Chi-Chi's one day
and fed her from his hand—Salad Tostada,
legend has it—then he was gone, but scents

of his Obsession and mousse gel lingered
for days on her goose-fleshed breasts
nestling in the hot-pink Jockey bra

his hands had stretched one size too big.
In time her belly rounded. Her parents grew
to aging strangers, not speaking to her

even during sitcom repeats. One night
turning from Dan Rather, her mother, livid,
looked back over her left shoulder and said

"This house is too small for us both."
Her father ran to fetch a priest, who tried
what lore he had to make her right again.

"*Nomine Domine*," he commanded, then tried
again in English, but all in vain,
and fled back to his suburban church,

clanging after him the simulated-brass doors
engraved with nearly every sin. Now she sits alone
in the family room with last week's *People*.

Rumor says he's somewhere far away, wasting
and mortally wan from thorns of remorse.
She won't buy it. She wasn't born yesterday.

They were not even what you'd call mixed.
Mothers from Little Italy, Peoria
and New Rochelle called to ask,
"And what are we to tell the children
once they read what you've done?
Better that a millstone be hung
around your neck. You're sick."
Women and men wrote to let him know
they were very thankful *their* God
wasn't dead, and if he didn't like
this country he could just go over
to Moscow or Tehran and see whether
the climate was any better there.
"And rhyme," they reminded him,
"was good enough for Longfellow."
His friends gave him too much room
walking and talking, and said that
while they knew what he must be feeling
he'd be better off from now on
feeling less where they're concerned.
Lovers recognized phrases given out
in passion—"Do it again, please, God"—
and accused him of letting too few bygones
be bygones, of every betrayal in the book.
Holding hands and nodding proudly,
his parents explained, "We're the ones
who gave him food, clothing, a roof
over his head, and college—

not to mention Jesus.
These are his father's words."
For the rest of his life no matter
how hard he tried to keep himself covered
when he walked among them, part of him
stayed unhidden, the chafe and ache
of nakedness his triumph and his shame.

4. *Journey to Calabria*

CHARCOAL SKETCH OF AGED COUPLE IN PEASANT DRESS, CIRCA 1880

Their child, Father's father,
took to sea in steerage
from wild Calabria, once a kingdom
ruled by nomad Normans, who

ages before their France
were Norsemen, fierce travelers
blown like cinders from bonfires
of home by prevailing gales.

In the eyes of ancestors
staring down the wall at me
as my hand makes its slow way
across this ruled page

I recognize a northern cold,
numb and alien unease
of wanderers huddled around
their frail, windy fire,

and at the same time
the sweet heat of storied South.
I find myself this night bound
to Ohio, where all that breathed

once huddled close in caves
as outside the glacier screeched.
I feel the earth tilt and lurch
in its incessant revolution

toward winter and beyond,
sky just behind my window
a map of the history of wishing.
What comings and goings lie ahead

for my own restive children?
I feel the family disease:
blood a few degrees too hot or cold,
home both before me and behind,

the need above all else to stay
and learn the lay and language
of this adopted land;
the ache to take leave.

AT THE HOTEL GIOTTO

On the road to Mount Subasio
across Spoleto's June plain

Umbria broods blue as a bruise,
blue as Giotto's lurid frescoes,

image and likeness made flesh
to bring passion back to church.

I must climb to make a place holy
as Assisi, walls that Francis,

sick of wars and fathers, made
to safeguard his unmilitant heaven.

Later, at the Hotel Giotto
on a brass 1930's bed there can be

only that earthly love he meant,
tolling of one brief eternity—

I lie alone; but beyond the terrace
keening swifts and swallows careen

their abrupt improbabilities,
azure dance of leaf and campanile.

In the basilica's lower church
mildewed masterpieces ooze

down walls soft as boneyard loam.
In my life's New World decades

how many priceless Stations
of the Cross have been lost?

"We're running out of time,"
Assisi screams; not in the usual way,

but running hard and far beyond it.
The city fathers now hold court

in what had been Minerva's Temple
and then a Renaissance church,

whispering place of tribe and empire,
leering barbarian and bishop,

Mussolini's bully black shirts
and gum-cracking savior G.I.'s

I couldn't stay any saint here,
divine hue of the merest art

glimmering more true than flesh,
every body to be embraced,

he very air a ceaseless cry
ne lifetime rendered sufficient

in its symmetry, canopied heavens
of swallow, lover's chill and star,

Umbria taking its own sweet time,
a poem of nothing more than blue.

EARLY SUMMER, VIA AURELIA

In Rome, I sense a catholic sadness
that rains on every procession, prick
of guilt at the tiniest pleasure,
doubts as difficult to pin down

as motes floating across the eye,
persistence of distant crickets,
teenagers revving motorscooters
through a city's gridlocked vistas.

What I'd give to be free as these two,
she licking his ear as he plows the Vespa
through storms of Roman traffic.
Giovanni and Maria, let's call them.

Seventeen, maybe. Hands under shirts
sculpt gooseflesh near Bernini's stone
in the Piazza Navona on Friday night,
Sunday kisses tonguing sweet mists

of Tivoli's thousand wanton fountains.
Even on the asphalt seas outside
San Pietro, the Pope's amplified blessing
in sixteen languages raining on them

as he bumps her rhythmically from behind,
her eyes closed, thinking the Irish nuns
standing nearby don't see him reach around
to madden the chafed, pink nipple.

They stroll the Foro Romano, monuments
to eternities of bureaucracy and sword
lying broken and moldly, Coke cans,
rubbers left by other night couples.

Maria, laughing, mounts the Vespa
behind Giovanni, clutches him with her knees,
smiles Madonna-like, as if she held
empire and liturgy between her fair legs.

They roar in fumes toward plummeting sun,
hair and clothing whipping wildly, youth
a lust to be in motion, a dream
to exceed this parking lot of art.

Tourist, semiofficial voyeur,
I can only wonder what Maria whispered
with swollen lips and tongue-tip
soft enough to make his back arch,

and what litany he kept murmuring
at her pulsing, proffered throat.
There was too much between us,
time and place, bursts of static.

They're gone, and at last I understand
my inability to hear. What kept me
from their songs were the cries
of the millions killed to make this place,

slaves who call to me now over shards
of power, wretches poor as urban dirt
who bore on their backs obscene weight
of Legion, Emperor, Duke and Pope.

Amid these neighborhoods of the stone
all passion hardens to—palace, basilica,
gallery—I can only ask *Whose fault, all
this beauty?,* and tell the wind, *I'm sorry.*

WALKING IN THE PIAZZA SAN MARCO, I REMEMBER ASCENSION OF OUR LORD ELEMENTARY, AND LESTER SHELTON, WHO WORE THE SAME CLOTHES EVERY DAY

To clothe the Creator in robes of gold
and dress up Mark's meager bones,
which their ships had stolen from Alexandria,
the Venetians loaded their church
with three miles of mosaics,
portraits of gaunt and haloed saints
dressed to kill; an enchanted forest
of marble columns of every hue;
constellations of porphyry and jasper
swirling on the floor, as many stars
as puddles and peasants in the piazza
after a rain; the *Pala d'Oro,*
altar screen of precious enamels
encrusted with 2,400 jewels;
and four burnished bronze horses
brought from Constantinople
when that city was forced to put on
a darkness stark as Cleveland's
in the depression of my youth.
For 1,000 years the Venetians worked
to make a heaven of their church

so that the best-dressed merchants
in the world, holding perfumed cloth
to their noses to disguise
the noisome scents of want and trash
in noon sun simmering in the lagoon
could worship with a magnificence
befitting their station.
To pay for the holy tolling opulence
Ruskin called "a treasure-heap,"
the Venetians sold Christians—
children, women and men—to the Saracens.
Did the slaves know anything of how
lives are bought and sold to make our art?
Centuries later an immigrant's child
comes to Venice with his own children
to look upon the stupefying beauty
and write this poem
for these betrayed slaves,
for the poor always and everywhere with us,
for Lester.

A RELIGIOUS HISTORY OF NAPLES

Back home, folks are too bull-headed
to believe the way folks used to,
daily grinding their noses so damn straight.
Here, souls still blossom with impossibles.

Within spitting distance of every altar
in this town there's an image or likeness
that belches, hiccups, whistles, bleeds,
sticks out its tongue or squeals like a pig.

In Santo Agnello, the mournful portrait
of Santa Maria d'Intercessione carries on
a heated conversation with a crucifix.
They've got a lot to talk about, God knows.

The statue of Santa Maria del Carmine
ducked her head to avoid a cannon ball
during Alfonso of Aragon's siege; still today
she flinches whenever that mischievous priest

cracks his gum. There too in olden days
the king would visit each year to witness
as the royal barber trimmed the hair
sprouting from the head of an ivory Christ.

Padre Pio, bloody pincushion of stigmata,
once took off planeless during a dog-fight
to catch in his arms the plummeting pilot
and tenderly taxi him back to earth.

No mortal mind can tell how many times
flushed and faithfully grateful women
are satisfied by indefatigable San Rocco,
patron of stamina and *coitus reservatus,*

and husbands send headache-prone wives
to the pretty chapel of Sant'Aspreno
to poke their heads through the hole
in his wall and fear the real darkness.

These peddlars pushing the sacred,
gewgaws, knickknacks, bric-a-brac, trinkets
carved from moldy bones of catacombed ghosts—
real and bogus—right beneath our noses:

they know it's a sure bet we'll put our money
where our souls are, no matter the rate
of exchange, to have this world miraculous again.
There's a wisher born every minute.

Even as I speak the black, clotted blood
of San Gennaro brightens like the Eastern sky
and oozes, bubbles, flows again hot as
our own, as we believers knew it would.

JOURNEY TO CALABRIA

I.

1 cm = 2 km, the map's legend reads,
a compressed life unfolding
until I'll never get it back

the way it was, time spinning
in roiling mountain coils,
wheel-whine, history's sheer veer.

Vision defies what little physics
I bring, dizzying *danza*
of plummet-rise, shadow-light.

I'm taking my sons to a land
too ancient and new for us
to believe, much less measure.

In a Fiesta from Hertz Italiana
we've labored in second gear
since dawn created Catanzaro

to hunker dark as ancient ravens
on granite branches over the Ionian.
Water and sky a spiritual *azzurro*

deep as the first blue I knew
in the New World, Byzantine robe
dripping with artisan's gold,

icon of Our Lady of Perpetual Help
I carried down the aisle
of Ascension of Our Lord Church

when I was still pure green,
a member of the Knights of the Altar
and the Future Priest's Club.

A childhood of incipient wishing
aroused by bourgeois art and song,
prayers for every impossibility,

even "the conversion of Russia"
we chanted for after Mass.
Can I believe that way again?

2.

The final incline into cloud
on the road to San Giovanni in Fiore,
no more than one hour,

as the crow and archangel fly,
from Serrastretta, the village
of light above twisted Edens

my family was expelled from
for the crime of too many *bambini*
of the wrong class on too little land.

Wildflowers blossom from skulls
of kings, crusaders, and criminals
buried among figtrees gnarled

like those bitter black *sigari*
the men would smoke outdoors
to squander hour after loud hour

at family feasts while the women
were left in kitchen and bedroom
to see to everything important.

3.

A wind of pine and wild onion,
peperone, basilico, virgin olive.
And did I once conceive of sacraments

as gifts that could be granted
only in a church? We pass countrymen
dressed for the peasanthood

that remains my legacy even though
I've been immured all my years
in middle-class wards and plots.

You can take the boy out
of the old neighborhood, not
the old neighborhood out of the boy.

Sullen eyes follow us Americans
in too-casual clothes, invaders
of a land whose ghost-ridden folk learn

to fear the stranger they'd sooner love
and feign the diffidence or fawning
that too often ends in bonfire:

rebellion, feud, revenge, *vendetta.*
The eyes of dark suspicion I see
in family portraits, every mirror.

4.

Beside terraced fields and roads
devotion murmurs from shrines
flickering with vigil lights

and tended lovingly as gardens,
death strung along the perilous way
like Stations of the Cross.

Portraits of lost children
look out at us, some of them gone
fifty years but still young perfectly,

endless calendars of saints,
Nicola di Bari, Antonio di Padova,
and especially *Francesco di Paola,*

about whose life it's still said:
It was a miracle when a day passed
without a miracle. So was I raised

to expect of each and every sunrise.
Grief at least, love's last work,
dies hard in these tenacious hills.

It's the worship of the dead
I understand, moldering bones
of pious fictions stacked like bricks

in San Pietro and the catacombs,
pelvic bones of alleged virgins
hidden in altar stones and crypts

the world over, perpetual adoration
of the dream that a life can mean
one moment beyond its sentence.

I've come to exhume Grandfather,
even though his body lies
20 years underneath Cleveland,

promised land he earned sailing
in steerage, striding B&O tracks
for a half-century of unlettered labor.

5.

In the speech, violin-wild,
I hear music of my childhood,
Calabrese dialect of Little Italy

and Latin of the Diocese of Cleveland,
the grand imperfect music
an alien can make of words simple as

Padrone and *Mamma.* My sons suffer
another speech about those who made
these storied heights before us,

Greeks and Romans, Arabs, Normans,
a family of heroes and brigands
whose lives I burn to tell.

Drops of their blood now simmer
with our own, I say. —*Sì sì sì,*
the younger one hisses, hoping

I'll soon run out of enthusiasm.
We've heard this a hundred times.
Please, not one more lecture.

6.

When the tire blows and throws us
hard off the side of the road,
it's a kilometer marker of marble

stolid as a tombstone and worn
like *Nonno's* calloused hands felt
all these years on my shoulders

that blocks our path, a crash
just moments from the mountain air
standing high over pretty Cosenza.

History. We've changed, I think.
Now the world's gone out of control
and I've forgotten how to pray.

I've brought children all this way
just to lose them? Ohio's hills,
less murderous, would've been as good.

Certain we're going over the edge,
I struggle to get back to the road.
Just before I look up at the faces

of the children who favor him
from where I lay stunned on the seat
and they cry *You all right? Daddy—*

I see again the old man's face
and hear his whisper roaring
like a railroad flare: *Paesan,*

my blood, my immigrant, you're home.
Capisce? And at last I comprehend
this journey, the ancient hills and seas,

and know why I've labored to make
a place where all my life I've been,
where, long as I live, I never am.

5. *The House of Memory*

HIDING THE SKELETON

A child, I'd hold my midnight hand
in front of the flashlight
that blazed like a railroad flare
or the torch of vented refinery gas
that laid the sullen city bare.

A nimbus of ruddy cloud around
each finger, life running crimson,
I'd see, clear as the old moon
making whole the arc of new,
behind the melting flesh, the bone.

At the shoe store, I'd be made
to step up to the X-ray machine
"to ensure a perfect fit."
Whose bony toes were those
that danced a furtive little jig?

What pretense, these years of hiding
the skeleton, his steady limbs
measuring out my steps.
For him it's the struggle to emerge,
outstrip the darkness of the flesh,

and I've grown old enough to know
it's my fate to be sloughed off
at the close of his long night,
old enough not to encourage him
by moving too close to any light.

ONE HUNDRED PERCENT CHANCE OF SNOW, ACCUMULATING SIX TO EIGHT INCHES BY MORNING

Snow billows over cracked blacktop
in parking lots of K Mart and Whirlpool plant,
plexiglass domed roof of Southland Mall
where young and old cluster and dissolve
in weekend conspiracies.

Snow blows over churches downtown,
each spire and arch shaped by antique disputes
concerning the shape or taste of God
obliterated now by tons of lovely nothing.

Here's my heaven: Ohio, bitter enough
to set teeth on edge and turn my face red
as litmus paper. Still, for all
our dirty profits, there's more love
than I can use, and more cold.

Near me beneath the ice run
the Olentangy and Scioto. So much
of our lives gets named by what's fallen.
I think of the ruddy women and men

whose teeth and bone lie arrayed in strata
beneath me, earth of their every fire dark
as obsidian. I step over burrows
where they weather forever's winter.
I'm coming soon, Grandparents.

My feet leave lines of script to mark
my progress, each step a fossil moment,
no two the same, lines that sing
my stride to anyone willing to follow

before this pure and ruthless beauty
disproves that I was ever here.

REDWING

Sentried on fenceposts
along Ohio 23, black backs
turned to steaming fields,
redwings cough warning
to raccoon and woodchuck,
possum, groundhog and skunk.
Coal-eyed bundles of fur
it took only the world
and all its time to make imperfect
lumber toward the glitter
of gravel and asphalt:
Turn back to burrow, to roots,
heated scents of family,
rut and pulse. Nothing
so unbroken, so monotonously man's
can do you good.
But the travelers haloed
in odors of ancient night won't hear,
move toward promises
of the next field, feast
of each tomorrow, and light.
Far off, beyond all sight
there's an incipient roar,
slayer of deer and field mouse,
its brutal weight and mass
having had centuries at least
to gain momentum,
its pain growing like the hell

that can take away entire prairies
overnight. For an instant
the eyes are bright as the stars
from which we all were spun.
Redwings chuckle as they breathe
one more time
the sweet stench of death.

FIFTY YEARS ON THE B&O, AND GRANDFATHER GETS A WATCH

Eskimos reckon five seasons
dependent on consistencies of snow,
tolling degrees of walrus-bone cold,
nights long as seals not surfacing,
blizzards hiding the whale,
each day a way of going blind.

Rain forest tribes halve
their years into Wet and Dry.
Aztecs counted thirteen hours of light,
nine of dark, each hour another god.

At sites of pyramid and megalith,
any cemetery on Memorial Day,
if we spend some moments on those
who've come and gone before
they'll keep time for us, counting
soft and slow as stone's erosion,
tick and pulse of every star.

Perhaps there are but two times,
then, which says *after* or *before,*
and *now,* riches we inherit
the instant they're ours to lose,
dwelling as we do on the border
between remembering and dream.

Now I'm saying this, but
in the telling it's all history.
Grandfather's each and every *now*
means me, his life ticking
from my wrist, glowing in the dark,
this moment my time for everything,
love's sweep of second hand.

IN THE KITCHEN, HE RECALLS A PASSAGE FROM SUETONIUS

He raises his fist high to strike
and the flashing flat of blade
smashes down pistol-shot loud
on the cutting board that bears the scars

of every last feast he's fashioned.
It's what he does. Wife and children
due home in two hours, in something close
to haste he's crushed the garlic clove

and brought to mind mad-eyed Giovanni,
herb doctor of Calabria, father
of his father. Memory's biting scents
for a moment make him old as fear

of dying unloved, take his breath away.
He scrapes garlic pulp into the skillet
to whirl and splatter in virgin olive oil
heated just moments from smoking.

He recalls that, in "The Shield
of Minerva," the dish that made him
immortal, according to Suetonius,
Emperor Vitellius served his guests

livers of parrot fish, brains of peacock,
lamprey entrails and flamingo tongues,
"Brought back in great ships from the Straits
of Spain and the Carpathian Sea."

He thinks, "So little taste remains
these days." Oregano and sweet basil,
calamari bubbling in sauce the hue
of heart's blood, goat's milk cheese.

It's a sacred duty, he believes,
the best we can do with this
our daily wanting, to season the one life
we're given and make the time to savor.

STARTING THE GARDEN, I REMEMBER THAT THE CITIZENS OF PURGATORY KNEW DANTE WAS ALIVE BECAUSE HE CAST A SHADOW

This April afternoon I've stooped
and stood beside my shadow
as our spades have broken earth
the groaning glaciers made.

Working just west of him,
I've matched each instep kick
and thrust, lift, twist, give.
A hard dancing we've done.

Now I'm grunting, sweat stinging
cracked lips, regretting
each pill-bug, writhe of worm-bit.
Weariness numbers my bones.

He makes no protest, grows larger
in fact as effort ebbs me,
evening coming to sweep away
the neighborhood's children.

Only wish sustains me: dream
of garlic, parsley, escarole,
dewy Romas bright as blood.
Between us we've nearly plotted

the garden, but I must rest.
He stops too, though I know
if I'd the will to go on
he'd follow all the way to night.

STAKING THE GARDEN

In Central America, the tomato—a weed of maize and bean fields—was to prove an extremely valuable nutritional supplement.
Food in History

I drive in the stakes
with father's hammer, and stoop
to tie to its wood each plant
grown wild already as a widow's child.
I stain my hands with the sweet stink
of earth, and all at once you're here,
Grandmother, eyes grackle-dark,
hair light as onion seedlings,
a dream of *pomodoro,* apple of gold
stolen from the New World, hoards
of Big Boys and Beefsteaks
preserved like papyrus truths
in Canopic jars, Romas sweet
with leaves of new basil and red enough
to simmer away Ohio's iciest evening.
Seven years you've been in the ground.
It's this laboring dance each spring
that calls you back, sweat
stinging my lips like
that first glass of Paisano on the day
you ordained me to be of age.
Together we'll make our way
down rows of this rich foreign soil
ages from Calabria's weedy, rocky sand.

Here the tongue cleaves to the roof
of the mouth at the unmusical speech,
no one believes in spirits
or the wisdom of the folk,
and too much tastes the same.
So I'll follow you in this caretaking,
counting each year with effort,
breaking ground, transplanting,
staking, weeding: earth even beyond
the grave our unfinished business.

THE FIRST POEM

for Mary

After the savage dance,
damp pant and thrash
yet splashed with grace,
the sweat of love
bitter as the spawning sea,
morning's vertigo.
Now the swelling.
Nothing tastes right.
No longer can you lie
or sit, the world
waits in embarassment
each time you try
to stand. Just being
becomes the mortal ache,
your hips bearing
the greatest burden.
The wait close to eternity
for the water to break.
How you hurt for the world,
backbreaking work
of generation.
Everyone around you
gowned and masked,
you moan out songs
that are beastly,
human, too true.

My hands
are on your shoulders,
your breasts.
We breathe as one,
the way we've been taught.
The treasure's unearthed
at last,
wrinkled and scored
like something dug out
of the Olduvai Gorge
but steaming like fallow fields
of April Ohio.
Life's wail emerges
from the cave,
light's flicker and flare,
seven pounds and three ounces
of the history of the world
fitting perfectly
our four hands.

THE NEWS

I'm pulled back into life
by precious babble from the crib,
my daughter's voice
evolving into art
an archangel's height
above the highest beast's,
her matins.
I bring her in my arms
down from heights of dream
to our new day.
This union nothing can rive,
I think, our lives
a double-helixed wish
toward what's good.
I place her in the high-chair,
turn on the radio
and go to the cupboard for her bowl,
unbreakable plastic
decorated with cartoon creatures
in chase and flight,
caught in what passes these days
for eternity.
The morning's a song
I've heard many times before.
Suddenly into the shuttered room
a voice skewed by urgency brings word
of "the third-worst massacre
by a single assailant

in the history of the United States,"
bloody prints smeared on walls
of an Oklahoma post office.
Though the unspeakable seems distant
here in Ohio,
nearly everything's changed.
Only the child singing
for breakfast remains untroubled.
For a while longer her perfect ignorance
will keep her from the news.

ON HIS DAUGHTER'S SECOND BIRTHDAY

One of those days
there's no turning back from.
Since dawn they've moved
too far, seconds together
a rhythm more precious
than any words.

What's between them
no clock can be put to,
wrapping paper strewn
around the room, frosting prints
on tablecloth dried dark
as blood. Theirs.

She sleeps now for tomorrow.
He couldn't be happier,
every moment a heart stroke,
systole, diastole.
The future closes and opens,
closes and opens.

THE FATHER
AND THE SON

I nick my chin while shaving;
my son bares his wrist,
searches for the rustiest blade,
sorrow pooling in his eyes.

I scold; he thrusts his hand
into ice, fire, calls himself
"Forever Second Best," climbs
the cross, singing "It is finished."

I grow comic; he invents love,
the erection, children.
He watches as I go ashen,
fall backwards into the casket.

We trade places; I bring flowers,
light memory's candles with
his last breath. We trade places.
This goes on forever and ever.

THE FATHERS

My children can't wait to leave
this town, their friends' fathers
home all week month after month
and dressed for Saturday,
getting in the way of child's play
and lusting after the wife
the moment she comes in from work,
mowing the lawn a week before it's time,
waxing the car until it gives them back
every worry line of one graying face.
The company moved to the sun,
or forced them into give-backs
until there was nothing to do
but strike, or laid them off
so long ago they no longer figure
in the unemployment rate
because benefits have run out.
They've quit looking, quit shaving,
quit counting the beers.
Even the dentists are up late
going over and over the books.
All my life I've lived among them,
Cleveland, Akron and Marion,
Youngstown, Toledo and Detroit
shrinking one neighborhood at a time,
roads south loaded with rental trucks
and pickups. Now their mills are cold,
machine shops boarded up, warehouses

rented out to artists and entrepreneurs,
mothballed ore boats secure
at river moorings, railroad tracks
stained blood-orange
with rust's rough patina.
To save money, St. Mary's
no longer rings the Angelus bells.
Three times each day I hear the silence.

GOING DOWNTOWN TO DRAW UP OUR WILL

This building's a generation older
than our first memory. The elevator
stutters, brass and cast-iron controls
calling to mind the trolleys I rode
as a child through Grandfather's city.

There's even an operator, in uniform.
She knows where to go. Her harsh hair
glows blue in this confessional light.
She stops one inch below the third floor
and coos, "Watch your step, please."

We read bad news in the plaster,
a corridor of cracks and failures,
map of where we're bound, man and wife
together. Finally, the frosted door,
Williamson & Sons, Attorneys-at-Law.

Just old enough, our sons know why
we've come, avoid our eyes, sink
into chairs and pretend to read.
The younger one looks up, eyes wide,
asks, "When will you be back?"

The secretary smiles, blouse white
as a Roman collar among cemetery pines,
as bond paper. I smell spices
in her hair, and carbon. As we step
to the lawyer's desk he rises

in front of his art, yellowed prints
of the Founding Fathers, extends his hand.
And I understand the family stories
of those Calabrians and Slovaks
who'd come to America to live forever

and with a last gasp sat up in bed
and stared each mourner in the eye,
or crushed garlic cloves or rosaries
with bare hands as they prayed
a mother's name in a mother-tongue.

And I know why, the instant
it's understood there's never to be
any more time, so many of us find strength
to dig in our heels, grab for anything
close by, and say *Not yet, not yet.*

THE SERVER

I'm the magician's assistant:
six beeswax candles twice my height
it's my duty to bring to flame
before the main event, cruets
to fill with Lake Erie tapwater
and wine from the pastor's stash.

I haul in the gilt-edged book,
the blood and smoke of centuries,
straighten the curtain covering
the tabernacle, God's face watching
from the other side, as critical
as any father's. It's time.

A man in medieval robes falls
repeatedly to his knee. I think
of Errol Flynn and his Sherwood men
kneeling the instant King Richard
throws off his monk's cowl disguise.
I've a new language ready, a cross

between the guttural Calabrian
of one grandfather and the Slovak
of the other, a rough-hewn music
in nasal accents of north Ohio.
Mea culpa, mea culpa, mea maxima culpa.
My right hand becomes the bell.

Industrial sun fires dirty windows
of Ascension of Our Lord Church.
Factory whistles hoot and scream.
Out in the parking lot, my bicycle
waits for the rush home, demons
gathering, dogs sniffing one another,

growls loud as the Innerbelt.
I'll ride wildly through thunder winds,
fearing a malevolent and petty heaven
that any moment could open up on me,
tongue still parched from eating God.
The demon in me will stir into thought.

THE MUSCLE OF GOD

I'm walking around in sensible shoes
on two bum knees I got trying
to outrun age, glasses thick enough

to distort light to fit an adult skull,
but there was a time I had no weight.
I moved effortlessly as an archangel

in medieval dress, pleated surplice
over the dark and flowing cassock
over the white J. C. Penney's shirt,

treading the sea of sacristy carpet
in spotless tennis shoes to fire candles
and fetch Erie water and cheap port wine

and speak liturgy in adenoidal accents
of the Diocese of Cleveland, while
adults made God again on the high altar.

Not even my mother could step up there
without calling down the holy fire,
and my father hadn't the Latin for it.

When we're children, we're so close
to miracle we can talk to statues,
all can be forgiven every time we whisper

sins to ordained strangers, and eating
pieces of God's muscle, guts, and holy bone
we can believe for a time we'll live forever.

FAMILIAR AS HOME

The sun, heavy as the cemetery's
bronze Doughboy, drops
into the ocean of sky beyond Ohio.
Last of the light flutters
on wings of ravenous nighthawks,
night no brighter
than the evening star stuttering
one hand's breadth above the horizon.
Fields of brown bean and corn
rattle in wind. Far off I hear
the cough of a harvester.
Angus stand snorting,
great heads shaking ponderously,
not quite ripe enough to die.
I try to recall how unaccustomed
to light I was in the beginning,
how welcome that first night
must have been. How far away
does the last one lie?
As I step across the fields
my body moves effortlessly
into the neighborhood of shadow,
a place familiar as home.

THE HOUSE OF MEMORY

after Matteo Ricci

We live in memory's house.

It stands on a proper street
in the neighborhood of *always was, always will be.*

Room upon ramshackle room of the wrack of stuff
that fills a life, things made precious
as they are.

Its walls still groan under the weight
of blizzard and August wind set to whistling
by the Big Bang of Genesis, bully cold and thaw
that gouged out the Great Lakes.

Grandmother stays upstairs
in a room at the end of the hall,
all garlic wreaths and Byzantine icons,

Lives of the Saints in Italian, mints
set out in a pretty crystal dish.

She waits for the nice young priest

to appear miraculously before her,
in his Medieval hand a vial of sacred chrism

to annoint her lips, head and feet,
unction a body merits only by going, highest holiness
in this fatal world.

The family kneels in candlelight
in the livingroom of early-American decor
as the black cassock passes by,
a shadow hissing out its mourning, warning,

on the walls
the picture of the Holy Family
posed devoutly on the lawn outside

their white middle-class suburban home in Nazareth,
and the photo of Pius XII, which reads:

The family that prays together stays together.

O bless this house and all who dwell
at 13605 Wainstead Ave., Cleveland U.S.A.

Mother, pregnant again, reigning in the kitchen,
face radiant from the pumice-rough love
she was born to, pushes back wisps of hair

with the back of the hand that grasps
the wooden spoon with which she measures out and stirs
our days. She sings:
O, mares eat oats

and does eat oats
and little lambs eat ivy.
The fragrance of her apron!

On this day O beautiful Mother.
Father comes suddenly in the door

after accepting Hirohito's surrender:

Lucky lucky lucky me
I'm a lucky son-of-a-gun;

I work eight hours,
I sleep eight hours, that leaves
eight hours for fun.

Hey! He booms out, *I'm home. Thank you Jesus,* the '56 Ford,
three years from being paid for, releasing
its heat in the strip of driveway separating
our kitchen from the neighbor's bed,

coat thrown over his shoulder,
tie loosened and askew. He smells
of the chemical company and carbon paper,

U.S. postwar prosperity. He's tough as Truman,
the world fearful of his clacking teletype.

I'll own this place in thirty-five years,

he vows, surveying the one plum tree
outside the screen door, rusting in foundry air,

that wheezes shut behind him,
Little Prince of the bourgeoisie
shut up tight in his castle.

I know the scents of this place
as clearly as my own,
air thick with damp coats, summer clothes
in mothballs, oregano and dago red,

childhood's glut of moments
ticking away like the furnace
just before the blower comes on

to spend precious breaths
of natural gas pumped up

from the Cretaceous period

that rages unabating in the basement
among childhood's boxed debris,

lumbering dinosaurs stumbling over new mammals
that scurry along the kitchen baseboard,
our earliest kin frenzied at the sexual scent of egg,

nimble and swift
in the new weather of their days.
Jungles of the past fall
to be squeezed into veins of coal

and a handful of diamonds.
Heat blossoms through the house,
dust drifting down to settle over

all the furnishings, what we've made of ourselves
by the time we must climb at the end of light

into the room of our very last dream.